D1536177

THE PERFECT THANKSGIVING

BY EILEEN SPINELLI

ILLUSTRATED BY JOANN ADINOLFI

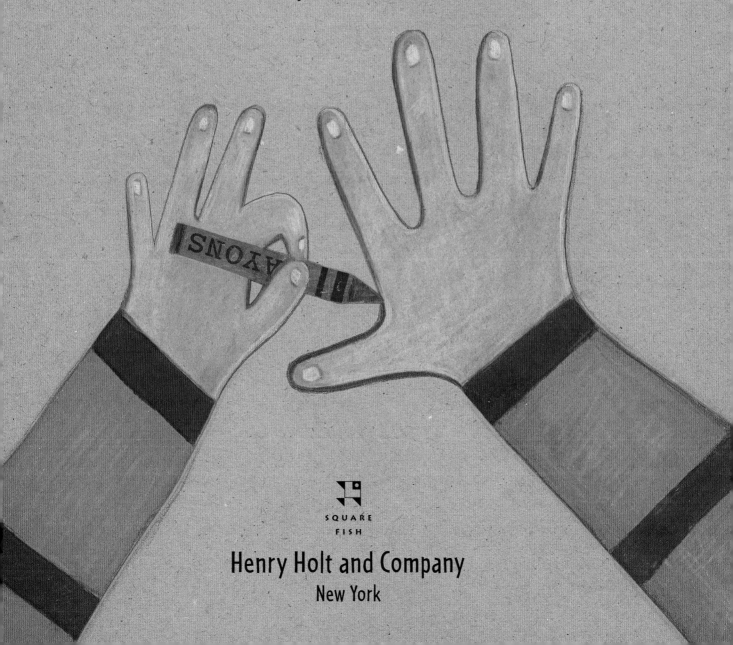

SQUARE FISH

Henry Holt and Company
New York

For Eileen and Jim Nechas,
friends for whom I am thankful

—E. S.

For Karsten, Hans-Liam, and
Gemma Sofia—I am thankful for you

—J. A.

HURRY!

SQUARE
FISH

An Imprint of Macmillan

THE PERFECT THANKSGIVING. Text copyright © 2003 by Eileen Spinelli. Illustrations copyright © 2003 by JoAnn Adinolfi.
All rights reserved. Printed in China by South China Printing Company Ltd., Dongguan City, Guangdong Province.
For information, address Square Fish, 175 Fifth Avenue, New York, NY 10010.

Library of Congress Cataloging-in-Publication Data
Spinelli, Eileen. The perfect Thanksgiving / by Eileen Spinelli ; illustrated by JoAnn Adinolfi.
Summary: Two families—one that is perfect and one that is far from it—celebrate Thanksgiving in their own loving ways.
ISBN 978-0-312-37505-8
[1. Thanksgiving Day—Fiction. 2. Family life—Fiction. 3. Stories in rhyme.] I. Adinolfi, JoAnn, ill. II. Title.
PZ8.3.S759 Pe 2003   [E]—dc21   2002010859

Designed by Donna Mark
The artist used gouache, colored pencil, and collage on craft paper to create the illustrations for this book.

Originally published in the United States by Henry Holt and Company, LLC
First Square Fish Edition: October 2007
Square Fish logo designed by Filomena Tuosto
mackids.com
·   5 7 9 10 8 6 4

AR: 2.5

Abigail Archer's family
is perfect in every way.
Never is this more obvious
than on Thanksgiving Day.

TURN THE PAGE
AND TAKE A
LOOK!

Their turkey is plump and golden.
Their napkins are made of lace.
Their table is lit with candles.
They all hold hands for grace.

Our smoke alarm is wailing.
Our turkey, burnt as toast.
Dad spills the gravy down his shirt—
a less-than-perfect host.

Abigail Archer's father
serves white meat all around.
Everyone takes dainty bites,
and no one makes a sound.

CHEW

CHOMP

My grandpa chews the gizzards.
My brother chomps the wings.
My sister slurps. My uncle burps.
And Aunt Clarissa sings.

SLURP

Abigail Archer's mother
wears organdy and pearls.
She decorates their homemade pies
with fancy whipped-cream swirls.

My mother's dressed in blue jeans.
Her pies are from the store.
Her Jell-O mold, a-quivering,
a-quivers to the floor!

After dinner at Abigail's,
after the dishes are done,
some of the grown-ups take a walk.
Others play chess for fun.

After dinner at our house,
the dogs sneak off with scraps.
Some of the grown-ups watch TV.
Others take long naps.

Abigail's older cousins
read books in velvet chairs.
The younger ones bring favorite toys,
and everybody shares.

My cousins chase around the house.
They grab each other's collars.
They hop atop the furniture,
and everybody hollers.

The overnight guests at Abigail's
have rooms all to themselves,
with chocolates on the pillows
and shampoo on the shelves.

Our guests bring their own sleeping bags
and canvas camping cots.
Some guests sleep in the kitchen
beside the cooking pots.

Abigail Archer's family
will sleep straight through the night.
They'll have the pleasantest of dreams
by starry window light.

My family fumbles in the dark,
eats leftovers galore,
takes bubble baths at two a.m.,
and many of them snore.

My family and the Archers
are different—this I know.
We can't tell peas from green legumes
or snails from escargots.

But we're alike in one way,
the nicest way by far—
alike in just how loving
our different families are.